THE BIG GOLDEN BOOK OF
BACKYARD
BIRDS

Text by Kathleen N. Daly

Chandler S. Robbins,
wildlife research biologist, U.S. Fish and Wildlife Service, Consultant

Illustrated by John P. O'Neill and Douglas Pratt
Cover illustration by Peter Barrett

A GOLDEN BOOK • NEW YORK
Western Publishing Company, Inc., Racine, Wisconsin 53404

Introduction

Birds have been around for more than 60 million years. It is thought that they first evolved from prehistoric reptiles. Today there are 28 orders or major groups of birds, with close to 8,600 different kinds of birds in all. Over 700 different kinds are found in North America alone.

Birds are the only animals that have feathers. A bird's covering of feathers—its plumage—allows it to fly and also helps to keep a bird's temperature even. However, not all birds can fly. The ostrich and almost 100 other birds around the world are flightless. This is due in part to their large body size and the shape of their wings.

A flying bird's body and skeleton are light in weight, even though the bird may have a long wingspan. For example, a red-tailed hawk may weigh less than 3 pounds, but it has a wingspan of more than 4 feet.

For years mankind has tried to copy bird flight with airplanes and other devices, but we have not been able to create a machine that either flaps like a bird or copies a bird's ability to move each wing and tail feather individually.

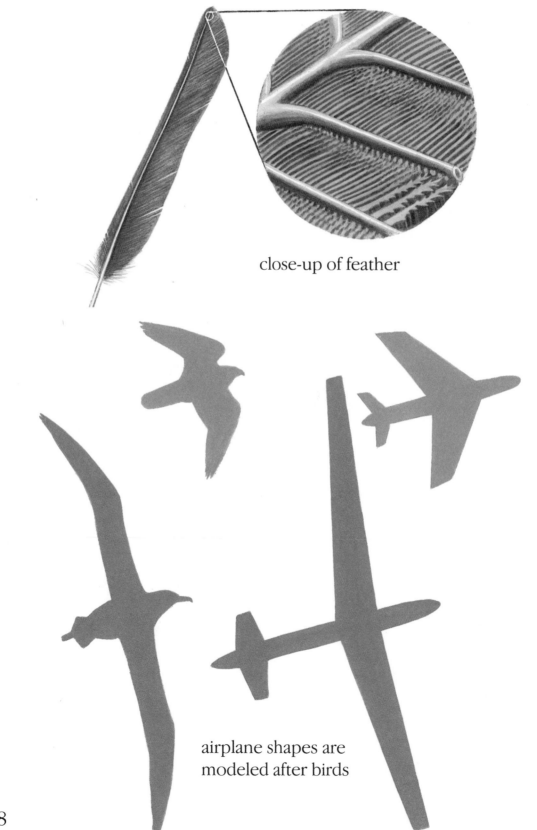

close-up of feather

airplane shapes are modeled after birds

seed eater

worm eater

insect eater

meat eater

Another aspect of birds' behavior that people have
studied carefully is migration. Migration is a journey that
some kinds of animals make as they travel away from harsh
winter conditions to warmer climates where food is more
plentiful. It is because of migration that some kinds of
birds disappear in the fall and reappear in the spring.

When birds migrate, each is looking for its favorite kind
of food. Although they have no teeth, birds can be either
herbivores (plant eaters), carnivores (meat eaters), or
omnivores (plant and meat eaters). A bird's bill often
provides a clue to what it eats. For instance, hawks have
sharp bills that can tear apart small animals. Finches have
stout bills that can crack open seeds.

Some birds can be recognized instantly by the color of their feathers. However, very often the male, female, and young of the same bird family will look completely different in color. For example, the male cardinal is a brilliant red, but the female and young are greenish gray.

Sometimes a male bird can even change its colors. The male American goldfinch becomes brilliant yellow and black in spring and early summer when it is looking for a mate. During the winter it becomes the quieter yellowish-green color of the female and young goldfinch.

Birds are so very fascinating it is no wonder that millions of people enjoy watching them. This book will help you become a birdwatcher by introducing you to–and giving you clues to identify–some of the flying birds you are most likely to see.

The major bird groups were determined largely by birds' internal features. The birds in this book are presented from the simpler to the more advanced ones. But if you want to find your favorite bird quickly, just turn to the index on pages 60-61.

Great Blue Heron

The slender blue-gray heron may be the largest bird you will ever see in the wild. It stands 4 feet tall and has a wingspread of about 7 feet. When it flies, the heron tucks its neck in close to its shoulders and trails its long legs behind it.

The great blue heron is often seen standing still or slowly wading at the water's edge, waiting for a fish or a frog to swim by. The heron stabs its prey with its long, sharp beak and swallows it headfirst. Herons make bulky nests in trees along with other water birds. There may be hundreds of different birds living together in a colony.

Canada Goose

The musical honking of Canada geese as they fly overhead in V-shaped lines is one of the first sounds of spring in the North. The Canada goose can be as much as 3 feet long. Its large size and its black neck and white chin coloring make it easy to spot. Canada geese spend most of their lives within a few miles of water, grazing in fields and even on golf courses. They make their nests on the ground, often on small islands in a pond or lake.

Families of geese may stay together for almost a year and the parent birds may mate for life. The baby birds, called goslings, can dive, swim, and feed themselves within a day after hatching from eggs.

Mallard

The mallard duck is the duck most seen on park ponds, often with a string of downy, speckled babies paddling along behind their mother. The mother and her ducklings are speckled brown and have blue wing patches. The male mallard has a handsome, glossy green head, a white collar, and a rusty-colored breast. Like many other ducks, mallards are often seen dabbling or tipping-up: They go head down into the water, tails up, to feed on underwater plants and snails. These ducks can also jump out of the water and fly straight up into the air with strong wing beats.

Turkey Vulture

If you see three or more large birds circling high in the sky, their wings tilted upward and not moving, you are probably seeing a group of turkey vultures. Suddenly one bird will descend and the others will follow. This means they have gathered together to feast on a dead animal. These large birds have a wingspread of about 6 feet and are easily recognized by their small baldish-looking heads tinged with red. The vultures roost in trees and may be seen over most of North America.

Red-Tailed Hawk

The red-tailed hawk is a large, heavyset bird with—exactly as its name implies—a reddish tail. It perches atop tall trees or poles and soars in circles on broad wings. Some people call the red-tail a chicken hawk, but it eats mostly rodents and snakes. It is found year-round in both mountains and open country.

American Kestrel

This small, brightly colored bird is often seen hunting from the top of a lone tree or a utility pole, even in towns and cities. It is the only member of the hawk family that hovers in one spot with rapidly beating wings. Its call is a loud, rapid killy-killy-killy.

Killdeer

This plump little bird is the most widely known shorebird in North America. It runs with quick steps, head down, then straightens up suddenly. It is easily recognized by its two black breastbands, longish orange tail, and loud call: dee-dee-deeer. The parent killdeer may try to lure a predator away from its nest of young by dragging a seemingly broken wing along the ground in the opposite direction from the nest. A predator may be fooled into thinking the wounded bird would be easier prey and follow it away from the nest. Killdeer are also found in open fields, golf courses, and even at airports.

Gulls

Gulls are large gray-and-white seabirds with black wing tips. They make the loud mewing or laughing cry that people all over the world associate with the seashore. However, gulls are often found far inland—on farmland, scavenging in garbage dumps, or soaring over city parks.

The ring-billed gull is one of the most common eastern gulls, and is known by the black ring near the tip of its yellow beak. The California gull is the most common inland gull of the northwestern states. All young gulls and females are spotted with brown and white.

Owls

Owls are birds that hunt at night. They have large eyes, flat faces, round heads, and hooked beaks. The typical call of an owl is whoo-whoo repeated over and over. This sound can be heard up to a mile away. Young owls sometimes give bloodcurdling screeches.

The screech owl is the most common owl found in North America. It is even found in cities. Like other owls, it seems to have no neck and can turn its head more than halfway around. This small owl feeds on rodents, frogs, fish, insects, and small birds.

The great horned owl is one of the largest and most powerful of owls, with a wingspread of about 5 feet. Its "horns" are actually tufts of feathers. It has large yellow eyes, a white necklace, and fine brown bars on its breast. It feeds on mice, squirrels, and skunks.

Rock Dove

The well-known pigeon of cities and farmlands is a descendant of the wild rock dove that nests on cliffs and other rocky places throughout most of the world. Because of their remarkable ability to travel long distances and then find their way back home, rock doves used to be called "homing pigeons." They were used for carrying messages from one place to another long before radio and telephones were invented. These handsome birds are mostly blue-gray in color, but some may be light brown or entirely white.

Belted Kingfisher

The belted kingfisher is an unusual-looking bird with a big head, a large, heavy bill, and a smallish body. You may see it perching quietly on a branch over the water. Kingfishers also fly low over the water and then suddenly dive headlong to catch fish with their large beaks. Kingfishers build their nests in long tunnels in a riverbank or gravel pit.

Hummingbirds

Hummingbirds are the tiniest of all birds. They are often brilliantly colored and have needlelike bills with which they sip sweet nectar from flowers. They are so tiny that they may be mistaken for large moths or bees. A hummingbird egg is no larger than a pea.

The wings of a hummingbird move rapidly, making a humming sound. The wings move so fast that it is impossible to see more than a blur with the naked eye. But slow-motion cameras show that the wing beats may be as many as 50-75 per second. Hummingbirds are the only land birds that can fly backward.

The ruby-throated hummingbird is the only eastern hummingbird, and the smallest eastern bird. It is only 3 to 4 inches long, and its weight is equal to that of one penny! The male has a brilliant red throat patch and a bright green back.

Anna's hummingbird is only found in the West. It has a red crown and throat and a greenish back.

Woodpeckers

Woodpeckers get most of their food by using their beaks to bore into live or dead wood for insects and grubs. If you see a tree trunk full of holes, you'll know that a woodpecker has been there. The rat-a-tat sound of a woodpecker hammering into a tree is unmistakable. The woodpecker has a very strong beak and a stiff tail that props it up as it climbs up a tree.

The downy woodpecker is one of the smallest woodpeckers. It is about 6 1/2 inches long. The male has a small red patch on the back of the head. Its back is whitish, checkered with black.

Unlike other woodpeckers, the common or yellow-shafted flicker may be seen feeding on the ground. It has a black "V" on its breast, a red nape, a brown back, and bright yellow wing and tail feathers when seen from below. There is also a red-shafted flicker, which has red under its wings and tail.

The well-named acorn woodpecker bores holes in trees to store its acorns. It is a social bird, nesting in colonies in oak and pine woods. You will know it by its flashy white wing patch and black and white colors. It is found mostly in the West.

Horned Lark

The horned lark is known mostly for its beautiful courtship song. The male flies about 800 feet high and then circles down, singing. At the last minute it plunges down to Earth, where it lands safely. The "horns" of the lark are tufts of feathers and may be seen only at close range. The horned lark lives in large fields, feeding on weed seeds, insects, and spiders.

Flycatchers

Flycatchers are known for perching quietly and then
making sudden fast flights into the air to snap up flying
insects. They then take the insects back to their perches.

Eastern phoebes are olive-drab flycatchers that often nest near people's houses. They are named for their frequent call, fee-bee, and are noticeable for their typical fly-catching flight—from perch and back again—and their rapid tail wagging.

Say's phoebe is a familiar sight around western ranches in summer. Its behavior is similar to that of the eastern phoebe.

Swallows and Martins

Swallows and martins are slender, streamlined birds that dart rapidly through the air, mouths open to catch insects. They change direction rapidly and seem to float effortlessly, only occasionally perching close together on wires or branches.

cliff swallow

The barn swallow is the only swallow with a deeply forked tail. Its back is blue-black, its underparts pale pinkish tan. It often flies close to the ground, twittering. The barn swallow makes its mud nest in a barn, garage, or other similar buildings. Swallows often return to the same nest year after year and are looked upon as a sign of spring.

The cliff swallow has a square-cut tail and looks much more chunky than the barn swallow. Cliff swallows often nest in colonies and make bottle-shaped nests of mud and straw. These nests can be found on cliffs, under the eaves of barns, under bridges, or in other places sheltered from the wind and the rain.

Purple Martin

The purple martin is the largest, darkest swallow, and is so adapted to human dwellings that it often makes its nest in man-made birdhouses. The purple martin soars and circles more than other swallows, and perhaps catches higher-flying insects.

Blue Jay

The noisy blue jay is a bright-blue bird with grayish underparts, a black collar, and a crest. Jays are aggressive and will drive smaller birds away from a feeding area. The usual call is a screeching, crowlike jaar-jaar-jaar, but jays also have a wide variety of more gentle calls. The blue jay is found in all states east of the Rockies, often in tree-shaded city streets.

Scrub Jay

The scrub jay is the western relative of the blue jay. (A few are also found in central Florida.) It travels in small flocks and has a noisy call. Unlike the blue jay, the scrub jay has no crest. It is named for the scrub oaks that it inhabits.

American Crow

Large, noisy, and glossy-black in color, the American or common crow is found almost everywhere. In wintertime crows roost in enormous colonies in tall trees and fill the air with their loud caw-caw-caw. These cries also warn other birds when a hawk or an owl is near. Crows eat all kinds of food, often foraging in fields and pastures.

Chickadees and Titmice

Small, plump chickadees and titmice are favorites with many people, because they are tame and friendly and love to feed at bird feeders, especially during the winter. They liven up any scene with their acrobatic movements, perching on the edge of the feeder with their long claws, or hanging upside down to reach into a container.

The black-capped chickadee and the Carolina chickadee both have black caps and bibs, white cheeks, and the same lively habits. They are eastern birds. The mountain chickadee of the West is very similar to its eastern relatives.

The tufted titmouse is the only small, completely gray eastern bird with a noticeable crest. Titmice, often in small flocks, feed along with chickadees, nuthatches, finches, and jays at winter bird-feeding stations. Like the chickadee, the titmouse is tame and friendly.

tufted titmouse

Nuthatches

Small backyard acrobats, nuthatches are trunk-crawling specialists, equally at home whether clinging sideways or head down as they search for insects in the bark of trees. Their long beaks help them to reach deep into the bark. The male white-breasted nuthatch has a black cap and white cheeks. The red-breasted nuthatch has a black line through its eyes.

Wrens

Wrens are small, very active brown birds with bubbling songs that seem very loud given the birds' size. They have slender bills and keep their finely barred tails cocked up over their backs at a jaunty angle.

The house wren is common from coast to coast. Bewick's wren, which has a white edge to its tail, is common in the West.

Mockingbird

The pale-gray and white mockingbird is one of the best songsters and may perform at any hour of the day or night. It pumps its long tail as it sings. The mockingbird can sound like other birds, a barking dog, a mewing cat, or even like a creaking gate. The mockingbird has long been a favorite in the southern states but is now found in the North as well. Its white wing patches make it easy to see in flight.

Catbird

The catbird is named for its mewing, catlike call. Like its relative, the mockingbird, the catbird can make many sounds. It is dark gray and has a black cap and a chestnut patch under its long tail.

American Robin

The familiar robin, with its rusty-colored breast, erect posture, and clear, caroling song is a well-loved sight to northerners. In fact, it is considered to be a sign of the arrival of spring. Like other members of the thrush family, young robins have spotted breasts.

Bluebirds

Bluebirds are North America's only bright-blue birds with red breasts. Like robins, bluebirds belong to the thrush family and sing sweetly. Bluebirds spend most of their lives within 20 feet of the ground. They drop down from their perches to catch insects and then return to their perches.

Starling

Sixty European starlings were introduced into Central Park in New York City by naturalists about 100 years ago. They multiplied and spread, and now these chunky, glossy-black birds with their waddling gait are found all over North America. After the nesting season, starlings flock together in huge numbers, often in cities. In the breeding season their feathers are handsomely speckled and their beaks are yellow. They chatter and whistle and make all kinds of sounds. Their noisy, aggressive behavior isn't much liked by some bird lovers, for starlings may drive away other birds, such as flickers and bluebirds.

Warblers

There are many different kinds of warblers. They are small, active birds, usually heard rather than seen, since they tend to like dense shrubbery.

The yellow warbler is one of the best-known members of the large family of wood warblers. It is our only small bird that looks bright yellow all over. The male has reddish streaks on its breast and sides. Its song is short and sweet.

House Sparrow

The chirpy little house sparrow is common in almost every backyard and city street in North America. It was introduced from England about 150 years ago and is therefore sometimes called the English sparrow. The English house sparrow has a monotonous one-note cheep. Flocks of sparrows roost in ivy-covered walls and often take dust baths in busy city parks.

Meadowlark

To many people, the yellow-breasted meadowlark—with its black V-shaped markings and flutelike song—means spring. Both eastern and western meadowlarks prefer open fields and plains, where they make their nests on the ground.

Red-Winged Blackbird

Once seen, the distinctive red-winged blackbird is hard to forget. Red-wings nest in large colonies in marshes and ponds, or in small groups in fields and along roadsides. The male has bright red shoulder patches and sings kong-ka-ree as he clings to reeds or dives upon intruders to his home.

Common Grackle

The common grackle is more of a backyard bird than its relative, the red-winged blackbird. It is noted for its big spade-shaped tail that goes into a "V" shape in flight. This large bird has glossy black feathers and yellow eyes. It forages in noisy flocks and seems unafraid of people.

Brewer's Blackbird

Brewer's blackbird is the common plain-winged blackbird of western roadsides and farms. It walks—rather than hops, as most other birds do—on the ground as it looks for insects. It is more common in the West than in the East. Look for the light eye and glossy feathers of the male.

Brown-Headed Cowbird

Cowbirds are inconspicuous blackbirds. They are most notable for laying their eggs in the nests of other birds. The cowbird eggs hatch first, and the newborns push out the other eggs. Then the foster parents raise only the cowbirds. Like other blackbirds, cowbirds walk rather than hop or run. Their plumage is dull, and the thin whistle of their song is not especially noteworthy. They can mingle undetected with other birds that feed on the ground.

Northern or Baltimore Oriole

The handsome northern oriole—a relative of blackbirds—was once known only as the Baltimore oriole. Its colors are bright orange and black, and it has a clear, flutelike song. Its nest is carefully woven of plant fibers, grasses, and bits of yarn, and is made to hang from the branch of a tall shade tree like a swinging pouch.

Cardinal

The cardinal is the only all-red bird with a pointed crest. It has a black mask and a short, stout beak. The female cardinal is light brown, with a reddish tinge on its wings, tail, and crest.

White-Crowned Sparrow

The white-crowned sparrow is a large member of the finch family. This bird can be up to 7 inches long and can be easily identified by its striking black-and-white head stripes, pink or yellow bill, and erect posture. It hops and scratches on the ground and stays close to dense shrubbery. Its song is a combination of clear whistles and buzzy trills.

Song Sparrow

The song sparrow is one of the most common and well-loved birds, recognized by its heavily spotted breast—with a large central spot—and its cheerful, distinctive song. It often begins singing on warm days in January and goes on well into July. It likes brushy places with water nearby.

House and Purple Finches

Both the house and the purple finch look like sparrows that have had their upper parts "dipped into raspberry juice." They sing beautifully, love to eat seeds at bird feeders, and flock together noisily.

Rufous-Sided Towhee

At first glance the large, brightly colored rufous-sided towhee may seem like a robin, but it is smaller, more slender, and has rusty sides and white underparts. It is a relative of the cardinal, and has the characteristic stout, strong beak. Its song is a cheery drink-your-tee-ee-ee-ee. Towhees feed on the ground, scratching noisily in dry leaves in search of insects or seeds.

Index